Tangerine and Kiwi

Visit the Bread Baker

To my father, the sweetest grandpa.
– Laïla

To my mother and my father, with affection.
– Nathalie

© 2007 Bayard Canada Books Inc.

Publisher: Jennifer Canham
Editorial Director: Mary Beth Leatherdale
Assistant Editor: David Field
Production Manager: Lesley Zimic
Production Editor: Larissa Byj
Production Assistant: Kathy Ko
Designer: Laura Brady

English translation © Sarah Cummins from *Mandarine et Kiwi: Le pain de grand-père* published by Bayard Canada Books in 2007.

Special thanks to Jean-François Bouchard, Paule Brière, Sarah Trusty, Barb Kelly, Curtis J. Pozniak (University of Saskatchewan), and Daniel Gonzalez (George Brown College).

We gratefully acknowledge the financial support of the government of Canada through the Book Publishing Industry Development Program (BPIDP), the Canada Council for the Arts, and the government of Quebec (SODEC) for our publishing activities.

 Conseil des Arts du Canada   Canada Council for the Arts

Library and Archives Canada Cataloguing in Publication

Héloua, Laïla

[Pain de grand-père. English]

Tangerine and Kiwi : visit the bread baker / Laïla Héloua ; illustrations: Nathalie Lapierre ; translation: Sarah Cummins.

Translation of: Mandarine et Kiwi : le pain de grand-père.
ISBN-13: 978-2-89579-122-5
ISBN-10: 2-89579-122-8

I. Lapierre, Nathalie II. Cummins, Sarah III. Title. IV. Title: Pain de grand-père. English. V. Series: Héloua, Laïla. Tangerine and Kiwi.

PS8615.E46P3413 2007   jC843'.6   C2006-906666-3

Printed in Canada

Owlkids
10 Lower Spadina Ave., Suite 400
Toronto, Ontario M5V 2Z2
Ph: 416-340-2700
Fax: 416-340-9769

About the author:

Laïla Héloua has given taste workshops to more than 2,500 children, training them to use their five senses and to care about the food they're eating. Slow Food Québec supports her work with children on taste education.

Slow Food Québec

From the publisher of

chirp   chickaDEE   OWL

Visit us online!
www.owlkids.com

Tangerine and Kiwi

Visit the Bread Baker

Story: Laïla Héloua
Illustrations: Nathalie Lapierre

Owl kids

Translation: Sarah Cummins

Hi. I'm Tangerine. My brother Kiwi, my mom, and I stayed at our grandpa's house last night.

Grandpa is a baker. This morning we're going down to the bakehouse where he's going to teach us how to make bread.

"Where does flour come from?" I ask.

"Flour is made from different grains," Mom answers. "Bread is usually made from wheat flour. We need to mix water with the flour to make dough."

"What is the salt for?" adds Kiwi.

"The salt makes the bread taste good," replies Mom.

"You also need yeast to make bread," says Grandpa.

"What does the yeast do?" Kiwi asks.

"It makes lots of little bubbles in the dough," explains Grandpa. "The bubbles make the dough expand."

"Are your hands clean?" asks Mom.

"You bet!" say Kiwi and I.

First, we stir the ingredients with a spoon and then knead the dough by hand so that it becomes elastic.

"In the bakery, I use a mixer to knead the bread," says Grandpa. "That way I can make large amounts of dough. But you can knead your dough by hand."

"You've each made a beautiful ball of dough!" congratulates Grandpa. "Now the dough must rest so the yeast can make it rise."

"What will we do while we're waiting?" Kiwi sighs.

"Mom, what was the bakery like when you were little?" I ask.

"When I was a little girl we lived above the bakery," says Mom, pulling out her old photo album. "The smell of your grandpa's bread baking would wake me up every morning. I would get dressed and run downstairs to have warm bread for breakfast."

Photo Album

"Grandpa was always covered from head to toe in flour. I could see his eyes twinkling as he handed me my basket of treasures. Every day we had a different kind of bread. Sometimes it was whole wheat bread, sometimes a sourdough loaf. Every so often, Grandpa put sweet buns or croissants in my basket. I could hardly wait to see what he had made each day!"

"Did you make bread too, Mom?" Kiwi asks.

"Of course she did!" answers Grandpa.
"Some mornings I would wake her up very early
and we would go down to the bakehouse together.
I showed her how to make many different kinds of bread."

"And before the bakery opened," continued Grandpa, "we would sit down together and eat our masterpieces!"

"I still like to make homemade bread with Grandpa," says Mom.

"Has the dough risen yet?" asks Kiwi impatiently.

"Yes, the dough is ready," says Grandpa. "Now we need to divide the big ball of dough into smaller balls. Kiwi, try shaping the balls into loaves."

But it's not time to bake the bread yet. Grandpa explains that we need to let the loaves rest a second time so they can rise some more.

Finally, it is time to bake the bread.

"Be careful. The oven is very,
very hot," warns Grandpa.

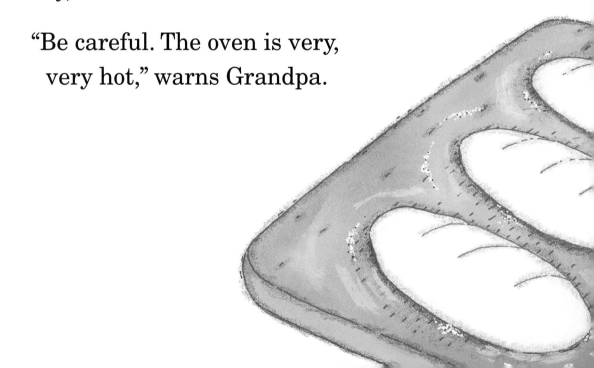

"**Mmmm!** It smells so good!" says Kiwi.

"I love yummy fresh-baked bread!"

How Flour is Made

1 Farmers plant seeds for winter wheat in the fall, and spring wheat in the spring.

2 In early or late summer, the wheat is harvested with a machine called a combine. The combine separates the grain from the straw stem and outer husk.

3 The grain is taken to a mill by truck, train, or ship.

4 The wheat grain is crushed, separated, and cleaned over and over until only a smooth, powdery flour remains. In the old days, wheat was crushed by millstones. Today, large metal rolls crush the wheat.

Different grains make different types of flour.
In Mexico, corn flour is used to make *tortillas*. Most bread in Germany is made from rye flour. Buckwheat flour is used in Russia and Poland to make little pancakes called *blinis*. Rice flour is used in Vietnam for stuffed pancakes called *banh trang*.

Grandpa's Homemade Bread Recipe

1.125 L (4 ½ cups) bread flour
415 mL (1 ⅔ cups) warm water
5 mL (1 tsp) salt
10 mL (2 tsp) sugar
15 mL (1 tbsp) baker's yeast
Extra flour for hands and work surface
Oil to grease the pans

1 In a large bowl, mix the salt and sugar with 500 mL (2 cups) of flour. Make a well in the centre.

2 Dissolve the yeast in 165 mL (⅔ cup) of warm water and let stand for 10 minutes without stirring. Then, stir and pour it into the flour mixture. Add the remaining 250 mL (1 cup) of water slowly. Gently add the rest of the flour, stirring constantly with a wooden spoon.

3 Stir vigorously for 10 minutes, then knead with floured hands until the dough is smooth and elastic. Shape the dough into a ball, place in the bowl, and cover with a clean cloth. Let the dough stand for about 30 minutes in a warm place until it doubles in size.

4 Remove the cloth and punch down the dough to release air. Place the dough on a generously floured work surface. Knead three or four times, then separate the dough into two parts.

5 Shape into two round loaves and place in lightly oiled pans. Cover the loaves with a damp cloth to protect from drafts. Let them rise in a warm place for 20 minutes.

6 Preheat the oven to 230°C (450°F). Five minutes before baking the loaves, place an ovenproof bowl of water on the lowest shelf of the oven.

7 When the dough has risen, make crosses on the top of each loaf with a knife. Sprinkle with flour.

8 Bake the loaves in the middle of the oven for 20 to 25 minutes. Reduce temperature to 175°C (350°F) and bake for another 20 minutes or until the crust is golden brown. **Eat the bread while it's warm!**